The KING'S Giraffe

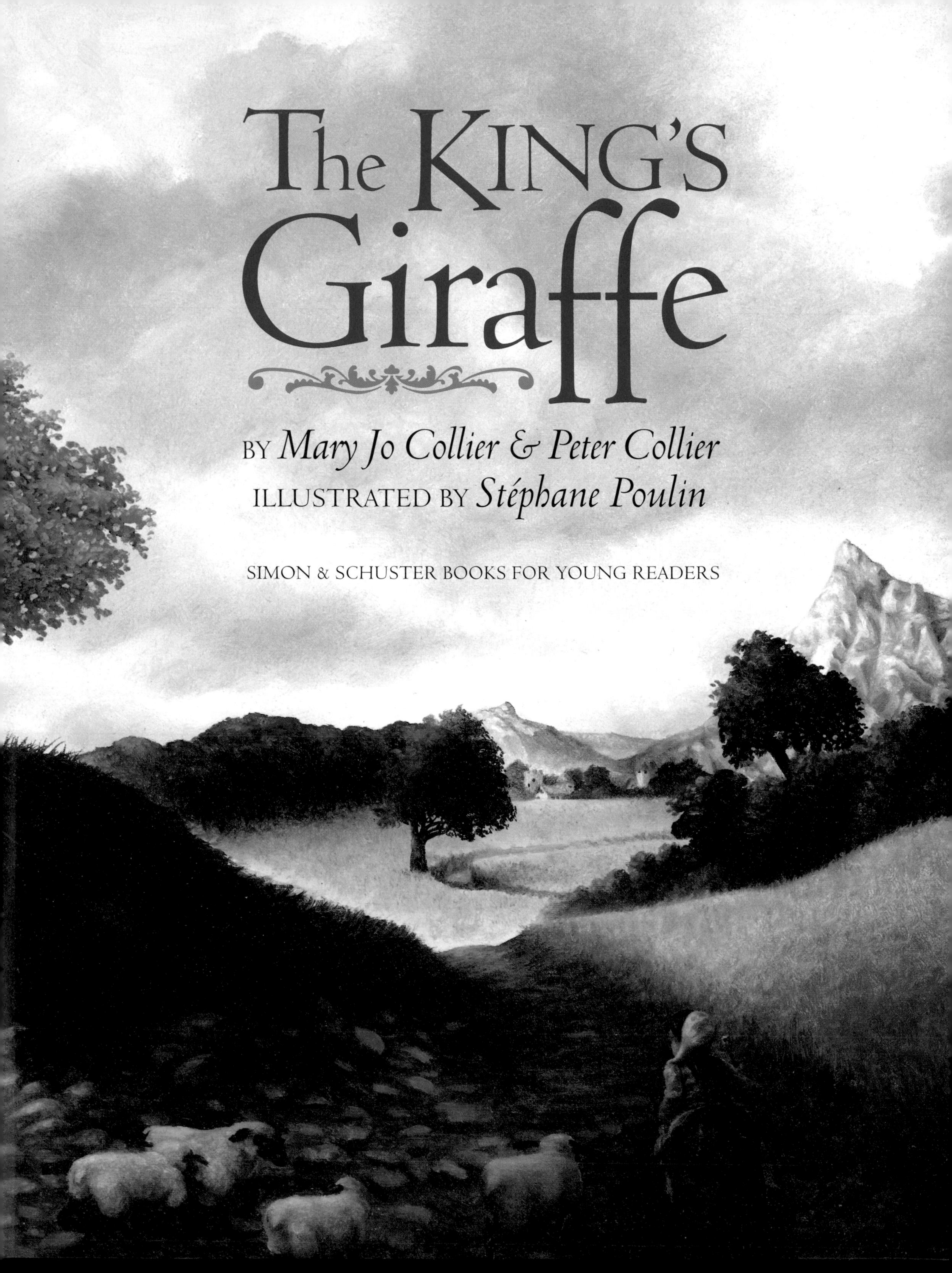

The King's Giraffe

BY *Mary Jo Collier & Peter Collier*
ILLUSTRATED BY *Stéphane Poulin*

SIMON & SCHUSTER BOOKS FOR YOUNG READERS

SIMON & SCHUSTER BOOKS FOR YOUNG READERS
An imprint of Simon & Schuster Children's Publishing Division
1230 Avenue of the Americas, New York, New York 10020

Book design by Paul Zakris
The text for this book is set in 13-point Goudy.
The illustrations are rendered in oil paint.
Manufactured in Hong Kong by
South China Printing Co. (1988) Ltd.
First Edition
10 9 8 7 6 5 4 3 2 1

Library of Congress Cataloging-in-Publication Data

Collier, Peter A.
The king's giraffe / by Peter A. and Mary Jo Collier;
illustrated by Stéphane Poulin.
p. cm.
Summary: When the pasha of Egypt sends his friend the king of France a magnificent giraffe, accompanied by its loving keeper, the people of France are awed and impressed, never having seen such a creature before.
ISBN 0-689-80679-5
[1. Giraffes—Fiction. 2. France—Fiction.]
I. Collier, Mary Jo. II. Poulin, Stéphane, 1961 Dec., ill. III. Title.
PZ7.C6795Ki 1996 [E]—dc20 95-22417
CIP AC

For Andrew, Caitlin, and Nicholas Collier. We hope they will someday enjoy reading this book to their children.
—P. C. & M. C.

To Camille, Gabriel, and Florence
—S. P.

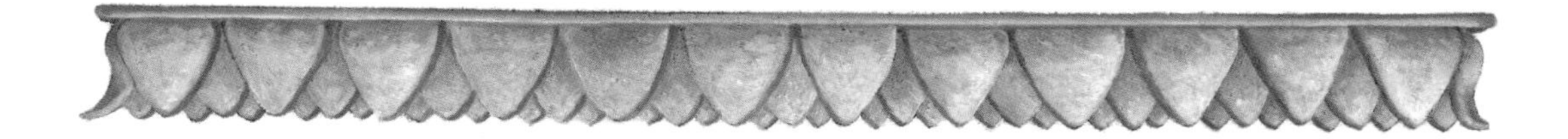

Long ago in Egypt there lived a man named Mehemet Ali. He lived with his wife in a grand palace on the banks of the Nile. This Mehemet Ali was, in fact, the pasha, the ruler of all Egypt.

One hot afternoon late in the summer of 1826, the pasha was tugging nervously at his beard and pacing up and down on the great veranda that went around his palace. His wife watched him for a while and then asked what was wrong.

"My friend, King Charles of France, has just sent a most impressive gift to our people," said the pasha.

"What did he send?" his wife inquired as she poured two cups of cool mint tea to refresh them on this hot afternoon.

"He sent a printing press," replied the pasha, who continued to pace.

"Can you imagine? Now all of our people will have books in our own Egyptian language to read."

"That is so," said his wife. "It is truly a very generous gift. But I must ask you then, why do you seem so worried?"

The pasha stopped his pacing for a moment and looked at her with great concern. "Why do I worry? Because this printing press will do such wonderful things for our people. And therefore I must find something equally wonderful for the people of France. What can I possibly send them?"

His wife thought for a moment. "You could send the French king your best Arabian stallion," she suggested.

"A horse?" The pasha shook his head. "No, not important enough."

His wife tried again. "You could send him your best camel."

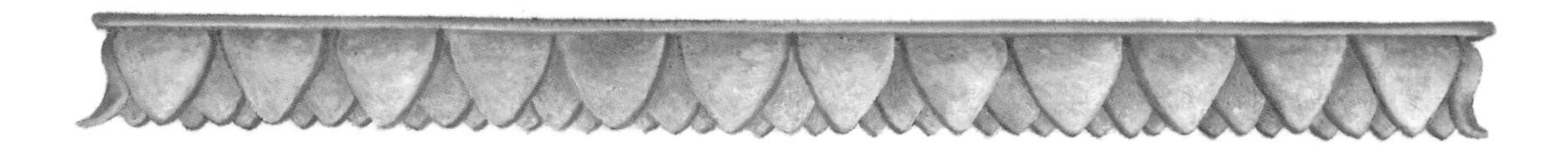

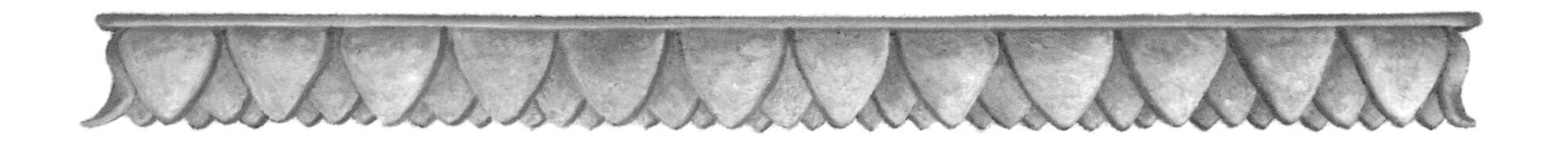

"A camel?" The pasha stopped and thought for a moment, and then shook his head again. "No, not a camel. A camel is not . . . not miraculous enough!"

Tugging at his beard again and sighing, he resumed his pacing. Now his wife was up and pacing, too, forgetting all about the cool mint tea.

Mehemet Ali was feeling especially vexed about this problem of the gift because King Charles was indeed a good friend of his. The two of them had learned much from each other. And their countries had learned much from each other, too. The king had sent many Frenchmen to Egypt to study the ancient pyramids. The pasha had sent many Egyptians to study at the great French university called the Sorbonne. Now the king had sent a wonderful printing press to Egypt. What was the pasha to give in return?

"The giraffe," a small voice said.

The pasha looked around. Then he walked to the railing of the veranda and looked out. His stable boy, Abdul, was playing with a scarab beetle in the sand below.

"What did you say?" the pasha asked.

The boy was very good at his job, and indeed seemed to feel more comfortable talking to animals than people. That was why the pasha was surprised to hear him speaking now. "What did you say?" he asked again.

"The giraffe." Abdul looked up and smiled shyly. "You could send the giraffe to the king of France."

The giraffe! It was perfect.

"Of course!" The pasha turned to his wife, smiling for the first time that day. "Of course! I will send King Charles the most wondrous animal on

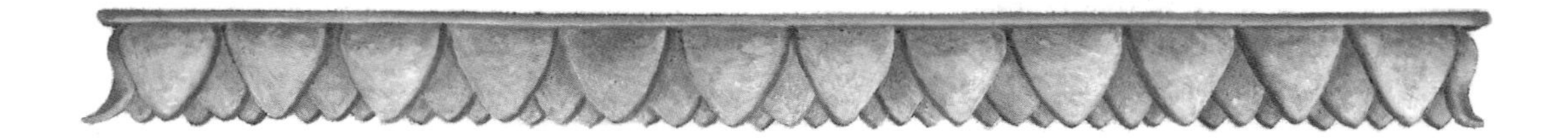

earth. I will send the people of France a present that will astound them. A giraffe! That is the very thing!"

This particular giraffe had come to the pasha not long before, as a tribute from an African kingdom to the south of Egypt, below the great desert of the Sahara. Mehemet Ali had seen many giraffes in his travels through the southern part of Africa, but never one with softer eyes or a more beautiful coat of velvety brown spots.

The pasha felt that there was something special about this giraffe. He was almost a work of art. He reminded the pasha of the carved figures found in the tombs of the pharaohs. He chuckled now at the thought of this wonderful animal arriving in France. The pasha himself had not been to France, but he had heard that the French were an excitable people and they had an expression they used when they were excited: *Oh là là!* He decided to go inside at once and write a letter to his friend Charles.

This letter said:

My dear friend Charles,

Oh là là, as you Frenchmen say. Please be expecting an extraordinary present from me to you. I am sending you and your people an animal you have never seen before. It is a giraffe. This present will soon arrive at your port of Marseilles. Please prepare a home for a most extraordinary guest. I hope that your countrymen will learn as much from this giraffe as we Egyptians have learned from the wonderful printing press.

Your friend,
Mehemet Ali, Pasha of Egypt

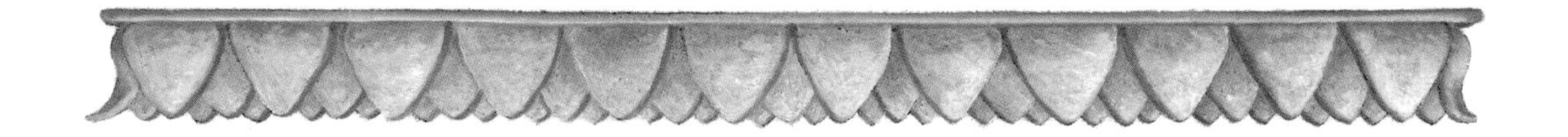

After he had sent the letter, the pasha had a sudden thought. Who would take care of the giraffe?

The pasha called for Abdul. He was about to ask him for his opinion about this matter when he noticed the stable boy looked downcast.

"What is wrong?" the pasha asked.

"Nothing, My Lord," said Abdul.

"No, you must tell me," the pasha insisted.

"Well, My Lord, I am concerned about the giraffe," Abdul began. "I care for all your animals. But this one is my special friend. I worry about him sailing alone on the ship to a land so far away."

"Yes, I worry about that, too," the pasha agreed. "In fact, I called you here to ask your opinion."

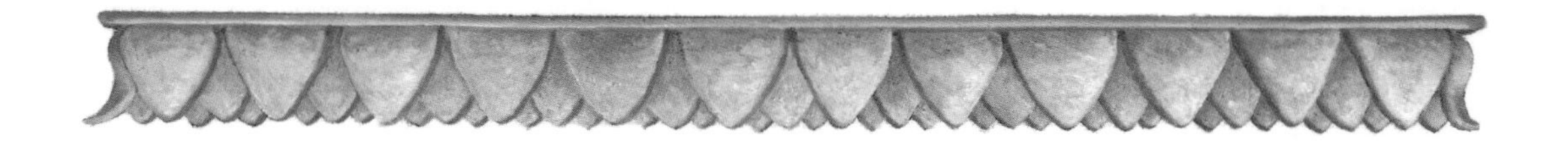

Before Abdul could answer, the pasha had another sudden thought. "Perhaps you would like to accompany the giraffe to France and stay with him for a few months until he arrives in Paris?"

"Oh yes," Abdul answered immediately, his face brightening. "I would like that very much."

"Well, good." The pasha rubbed his hands together. "It is settled then."

After weeks of preparation, Mehemet Ali and his court traveled to the Egyptian port city of Alexandria with Abdul and the giraffe. Even though the giraffe ate leaves, it had been determined that the animal would drink milk during the long voyage to Marseilles. Abdul had calculated that the wondrous animal would require twenty-five liters a day. Just before the ship was to sail, he went to the pasha.

"Sire, I am afraid that the ship will not be able to store enough milk," he said.

The pasha rubbed his beard and thought for a moment. "I know!" he said. "We will get three cows that will produce milk every day and also keep the giraffe company."

After the three cows had been loaded, Mehemet Ali and his party watched Abdul lead the giraffe up the gangplank onto the ship. The pasha and his party waved their handkerchiefs as the ship sailed off.

Fortunately, the voyage was fairly calm and only the milk cows got a little seasick, which meant that for several days they produced buttermilk. Abdul spent time stroking the giraffe's long, graceful neck to keep him from being frightened. The stable boy made sure that the giraffe's bedding was soft and clean.

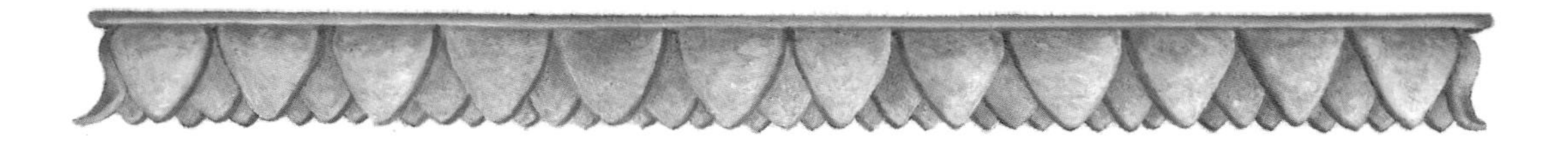

Abdul sang songs each night to pass the time. The giraffe allowed the stable boy to lay his head against its velvety stomach, and often Abdul went to sleep listening to the gentle creature's heartbeat. As the ship rocked softly on the waves, he dreamed of his homeland.

As they neared Marseilles, the ship's crew became more and more excited. They practiced their French by saying all together, "*Oh là là!*"

Abdul went below to groom the giraffe. He was happily brushing the animal's coat and polishing his hooves when he heard the gangplank hit the dock with a thud. He got ready to set foot on French soil with the giraffe.

What a sight! There were people everywhere, more people than he had ever seen in one place. *Oh là là*s filled the air. And the smells! There were

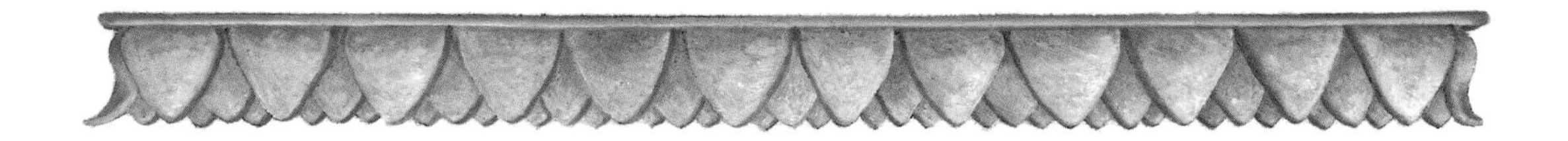

women on the dock cooking great cauldrons of bouillabaisse, which they were serving to all of the people who had come to welcome the giraffe to France. There were bakers wheeling wheelbarrows full of loaves of long French bread. Then Abdul saw a group of men approach the gangplank. They rolled out a specially woven Turkish carpet so that the giraffe's first steps on French soil would be as soft as walking in the grass of Africa.

The mayor of Marseilles raised his hand to quiet the crowd, and then he climbed a ladder held up by four men so that he could speak directly to the giraffe. "Monsieur Giraffe, I welcome you to France," said the mayor in a loud and official-sounding voice. "The people of Marseilles are honored to have you as a guest. We invite you to spend the winter with us before you leave for the great city of Paris and your new home in the Royal Menagerie of the king."

Suddenly, several girls and boys pushed their way through the crowd. They had made the giraffe an immense cape of red brocade!

"France can be very cold," the mayor explained, and then he helped Abdul tie the cape around the giraffe's neck with red satin ribbons. When they finished, the crowd began to applaud and shout, "*Vive la girafe!*"

The townspeople of Marseilles escorted Abdul and the giraffe to the mayor's house. The mayor's wife hurried out to greet them, wiping her hands on her apron, and led them around to the back of the house, through the garden, and past the rabbit cages into the barn. The mayor had already gotten workers to remove a part of the roof to make room for his very tall houseguest. "*Voilà!*" said the mayor's wife as she pointed to Abdul and the giraffe's new quarters, and the sight of this very small Frenchwoman next to the very tall giraffe made the stable boy smile.

LAVANDIÈRE
ANIS
BOIS
BOULANGERIE
CRÉMERIE
MAITRE VOILIER FILS

VINS
CAFÉ DE LA MARINE
CAFÉ
VIN
CAFÉ
AVIS

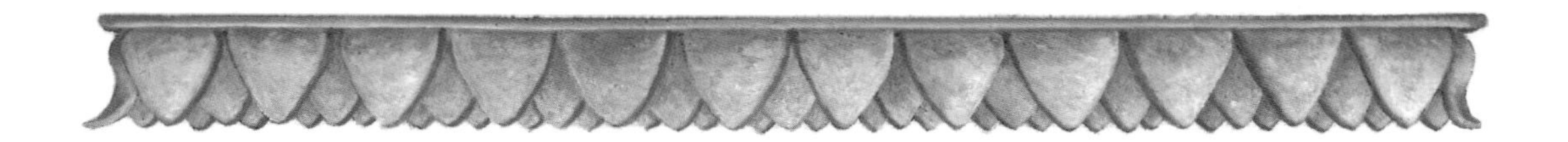

Over the next few weeks the townspeople of Marseilles came to love the giraffe. They kept calling him "our" giraffe and saying things like "Our giraffe must have the longest neck of any giraffe in the world." When they heard that their guest liked milk, they made sure that foamy buckets of fresh milk arrived each morning at the mayor's barn. Schoolchildren would stop by on the way to school, shouting *"Bonjour!"* to Abdul and bringing little candy treats for the giraffe. Some of them brought the first new carrots from their mothers' gardens and watched the giraffe, which made few other noises, crunch them in his mouth.

Sometimes when Abdul woke up in the morning and looked out of the barn window, he would see people gathered. They would be pointing up at the giraffe's long neck, which poked out of the open spot in the roof.

Every day after work the mayor would hurry home from his office. After changing his clothes, he would come out to the barn and sit talking with Abdul, sometimes standing on a ladder to rub his cheek against the giraffe's soft coat. He told Abdul about Paris, a city of tall buildings and wide boulevards. Then he began to teach Abdul how to speak and write French. Abdul learned to count—*un, deux, trois*. He learned the names of the colors—*rouge*, red like the cape; *jaune*, yellow like the giraffe's smooth coat; *brun*, the brown of its spots.

After the French lessons, it was Abdul's turn to teach the mayor. He told him stories about the land of camels and pyramids. He told the mayor about the southern part of Africa below the Sahara desert, the

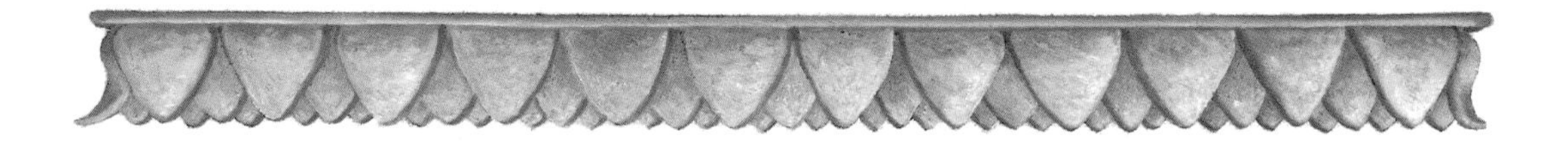

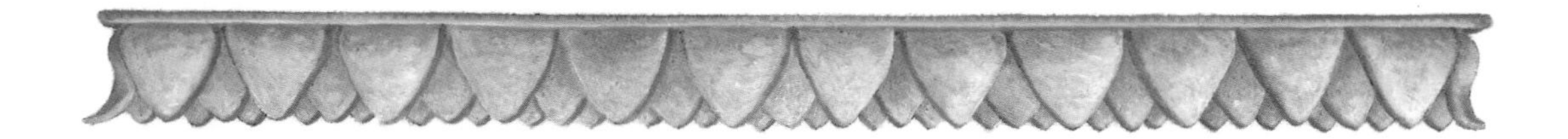

great grassy plains where the giraffe had lived with elephants and rhinoceroses and lions and leopards.

"*Sacré bleu!*" whispered the mayor.

And so the winter passed. There were some days that were difficult for Abdul because the wind blew so hard and he was so far from home. But then the wind would stop and there would be an incredible night, clear and still, with the stars blazing like diamonds on black satin. Abdul would lay beside the giraffe in the stall. Resting his head against the animal's soft side, he listened to the giraffe's heartbeat as he drifted off to sleep.

And then one day it seemed that all at once the smell of spring was in the air. Wild lavender began to bloom on the hillsides around Marseilles. The flowers' spicy scent mingled with the sweetness of the cherry blos-

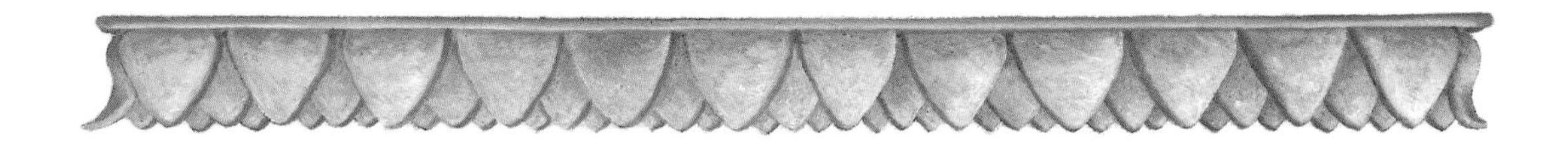

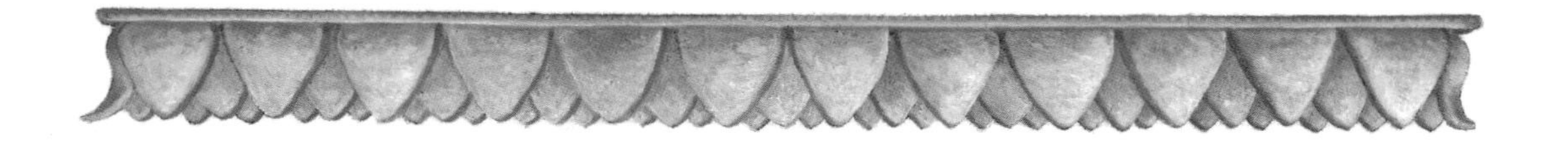

soms in the mayor's garden. The twentieth of May was set as the day they would leave for Paris.

"Don't forget to make our friend wear his red cape," said the mayor's wife as she packed a basket of food for the giraffe. "The nights are still chilly."

The people of Marseilles lined the avenue that ran past the mayor's house and out of town. "*Bon voyage!*" said the mayor, dabbing at his cheeks with a handkerchief. "*Adieu!*" cried the crowd as Abdul and the giraffe passed by, leading the entourage the mayor had ordered to accompany them to Paris. Mothers threw flowers in their path and said, "*Au revoir!*" Fathers held up their babies so that the children could say later that they had seen the first giraffe ever to set foot in France.

Abdul and the giraffe and their entourage spent the first night in Aix-en-Provence. It was the perfect city for a giraffe. Cours Mirabeau was a shady, tree-lined avenue that led straight through the city. The giraffe nibbled his way first down one side and then up the other while the French foreign legion band played the "Marseillaise." Abdul walked proudly beside the giraffe and practiced his French.

"*Quelle magnifique!*" an old man said as they passed by.

"Yes," said Abdul, "the giraffe is magnificent." This was something that a Frenchman and an Egyptian could certainly agree on.

In Avignon all of the children in town gathered in the Place de l' Horloge to sing a special song to the giraffe, which they sang to the tune of "Sur la Pont d'Avignon." This is what they sang:

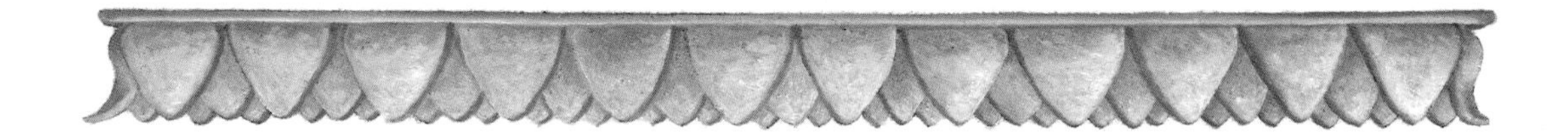

Sur la place c'est une girafe
Bienvenue, Bienvenue
Sur la place, c'est une girafe
C'est la première dans toute la France.

By this time, Abdul knew enough French so that he could understand pretty much what all the words meant.

In our plaza there is a giraffe
Welcome, welcome
In our plaza there is a giraffe
It is the first one in all of France.

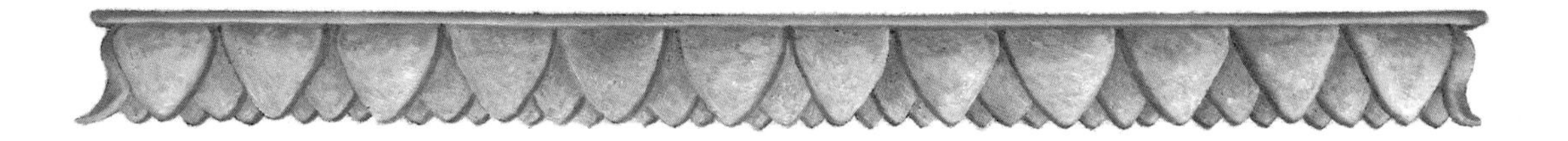

It was June by the time they reached Lyon. There were already hundreds of people waiting. "*Voilà!*" the crowd gasped as the giraffe came into view. The great writer Stendhal began his welcoming speech with one word: *Extraordinaire!* Many restaurants in Lyon created new dishes to honor the giraffe.

And so it was in every town they entered. The people would gather to wait and watch. And then the giraffe would come into view, his long, stately stride making it seem as though he floated rather than walked.

In Dijon, a town famous for its spicy mustard, the giraffe arrived very thirsty. In the middle of the welcoming ceremonies in the town square, he stopped paying attention and began to stare at a nearby fountain. Then he slowly spread his front legs and slowly lowered his long neck and began to drink. As he did this, the speakers stopped speaking and the band stopped playing. Everyone watched as the giraffe raised his head so that the mouthfuls of water could slide down his throat. This time the crowd did not say, "*Oh là là!*" It just said, "*Ohhhhhhhh.*"

Finally, after six weeks of walking almost the entire length of France and making friends everywhere they stopped, Abdul and the giraffe and their entourage arrived at the edge of Paris. They were told that King Charles had been waiting with great anticipation all winter for his guest.

In fact, his entire court had been engaged in a whirlwind of preparation. The royal gardener had even traveled to Holland to choose the most spectacular late-blooming yellow and golden brown tulips in honor of the giraffe's coat, and ten assistants had helped him plant them in the Jardin des Plantes.

The Jardin des Plantes was the king's own royal garden. Neat planting beds were filled with medicinal herbs and fragrant roses. Greenhouses con-

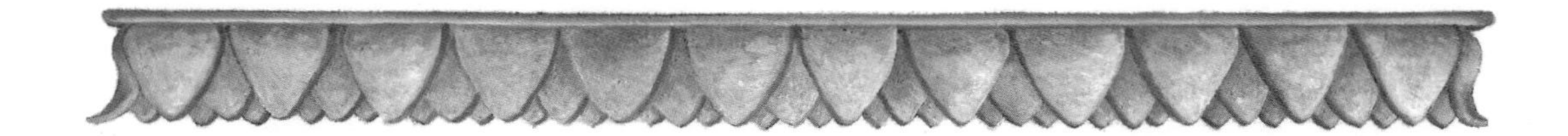

tained strange tropical plants gathered by Frenchmen in their travels to the four corners of the world. And just beyond was the Royal Menagerie, where the greatest collection of exotic animals in all Europe lived.

King Charles loved to spend time here with his grandson Henry. They would wander along the gravel paths and sit on the iron benches under the plane trees. They would eat delicate sorbets made from the fruit grown on the trees in the garden. All winter long, while the giraffe was staying in Marseilles, Henry listened to his grandfather, the king, practice the speech he was going to make when the giraffe finally arrived.

During the time in which the king was practicing his speech, the royal clothes designer was creating new gowns for the ladies of the court, gowns with high collars that were intended to make their wearers' necks look

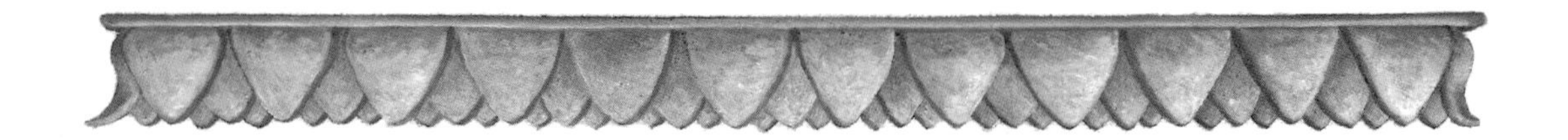

long and thin. The royal poets were creating long, thin poems in honor of the long, thin guest that would soon be with them. Even the king's hatmaker got into the act, producing a rather strange creation with two knobs sticking up out of the top and something that looked like giraffe ears flopping out from the sides. All of Paris was in a tizzy.

Now the big moment was finally at hand. The king's messengers ran ahead to Saint-Cloud, where the king had his summer chateau, to tell him that the giraffe had arrived. After they had gone, Abdul settled the giraffe down for their last night together. He listened to the quiet breathing of the giraffe and thought about all they had seen together since landing in France.

Abdul had a moment of doubt the next morning. What if King Charles, good friend of the pasha, did not recognize the beauty of this animal? What if he was disappointed after the long months of anticipation? Abdul pushed these thoughts out of his mind and continued to prepare his friend for what he expected would be their final good-bye.

"I'm sorry to leave you," Abdul said as he brushed the giraffe's gleaming coat. "But you can't expect the king of France to have any need of a stable boy." The giraffe swung his head down and looked curiously at Abdul.

No sooner had Abdul finished the grooming than the king's messengers arrived to say that he should now come and present the giraffe at Saint-Cloud.

When they arrived, King Charles himself was standing just inside the ornate iron gates with his grandson Henry. They both had their hands

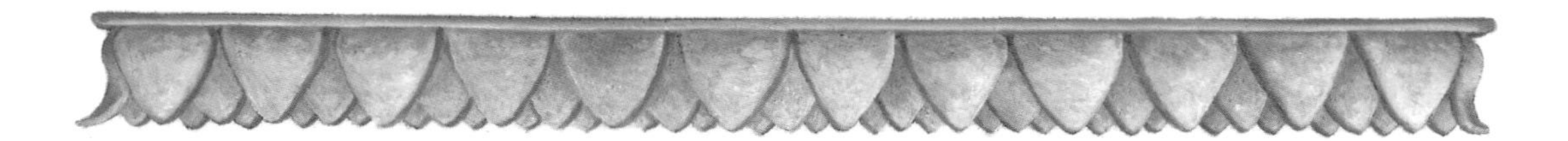

over their eyes to keep up the suspense until the last moment. When they at last took their hands down, they stood there with their eyes opened wide in wonderment.

There was a hush as everyone waited for the welcoming speech the king had been practicing all winter, but the king was speechless. After a few moments, his face grew red with embarrassment, because the words would not come to him. Then his little grandson Henry stepped forward and in a tiny, shaking voice gave the speech that he had heard his grandfather practice so many times.

"Welcome to your new home," he said, holding his head far back so as to see the giraffe's face while he spoke. "The people of France wish to bestow upon you this medal of honor for being the first giraffe ever to come to France."

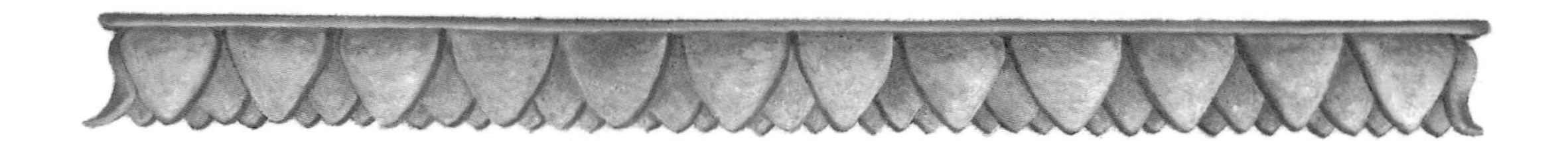

At this, some royal workmen appeared with a scaffolding, and little Henry climbed up to tie the medal, which was in the shape of a giraffe, around the animal's neck. The crowd cheered and shouted, *"Vive la girafe!"*

King Charles finally came out of his daze and shook Abdul's hand. Then he turned to the crowd and said in a loud and official voice, "Everyone is invited to the Jardin des Plantes for profiteroles!"

The king's trumpeters tooted their horns for the grand march to the Royal Menagerie to begin. And march they did. All of the cadets from the École Militaire had lined up in columns of six to escort the giraffe. Small girls and boys waved miniature French flags, while bigger boys and girls climbed up into the chestnut trees that lined the streets so that they could catch an early glimpse of the royal giraffe.

They passed through the Tuileries. They crossed over the Pont Neuf and stopped in front of the church of St.-Sulpice, where the priest gave the giraffe a special blessing for a long life. They stopped to rest in the Jardin de Luxembourg, and there they watched a special puppet show performed for all the children who had waited so long and so patiently for the arrival of the giraffe.

Finally, everyone arrived at the Jardin des Plantes and made their way along the paths that bordered planting beds full of thyme and rosemary and mint. Abdul couldn't believe the size of the greenhouses, which weren't green at all but made of glass and filled with people. As they came to the buildings that made up the Royal Menagerie, all the other animals that lived there looked up from their midday meal in astonishment at the uproar the giraffe was causing. However, as soon as the giraffe

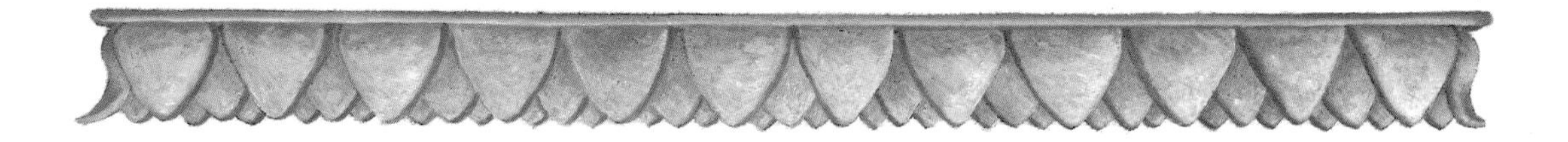

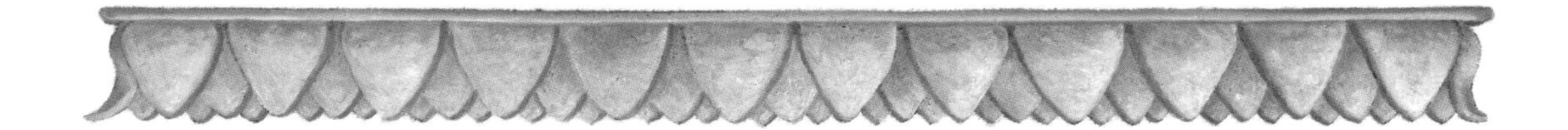

was settled in his new enclosure, the other animals began to feel drowsy, and one by one they dropped off for their afternoon nap.

There was much feasting and celebrating that afternoon in the Jardin des Plantes. Everyone ate profiteroles. The ladies of the court paraded around in their new gowns and silly hats. The king's grandson Henry was so excited by the success of the brief speech he had made to the crowd that he spent the rest of the day riding the stick giraffe that the royal toymaker had made for him and giving the speech again to anyone who would listen.

Abdul was very happy, too. All of the Egyptian students from the Sorbonne had been invited to the festivities. They began by speaking

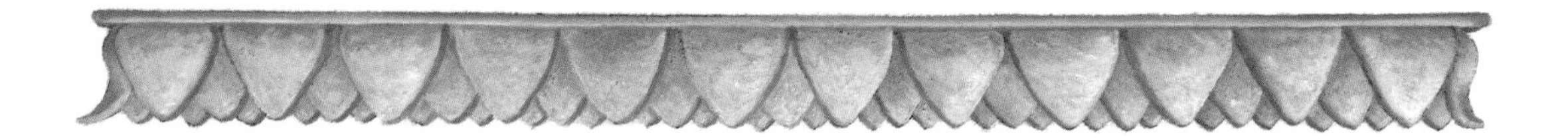

French to one another and then, realizing that they were Egyptians after all, they began to speak Egyptian.

The glorious day ended with royal fireworks bursting in the sky. But Abdul missed them because he had gone to check on the giraffe. He thought his friend might be lonely in his new home.

He was standing beside the giraffe, stroking the wondrous coat, when he sensed someone beside him. Abdul turned and saw King Charles, alone and without any of his servants. The king smiled at him and then reached out a hand and shyly began to pet the giraffe, too. He and Abdul stood side by side for a while, each petting the giraffe. The king was thinking that he had much to learn, not only from the giraffe, but from Abdul, who could teach even French naturalists much about a place like Africa, which had such exotic plants and animals. And Abdul was thinking that he would still like to learn more French words and perhaps have a little garden where he could grow different varieties of carrots and lettuces, which the giraffe loved to eat.

"Excuse me." The king finally cleared his throat and began to speak. "Perhaps you could do me a great favor. My friend the pasha of Egypt has written me about you. He says that you are a special person. The giraffe and all the other animals here need a special friend, someone who understands them and who can, in a manner of speaking, communicate with them. It is a job for a special person. I know it would be a great inconvenience to you, Monsieur Abdul, but I was thinking that perhaps you would stay with us for a while and be the keeper of the Royal Menagerie."

Abdul's heart thumped with excitement. He would have a chance to stay with the giraffe! As keeper of the Royal Menagerie!

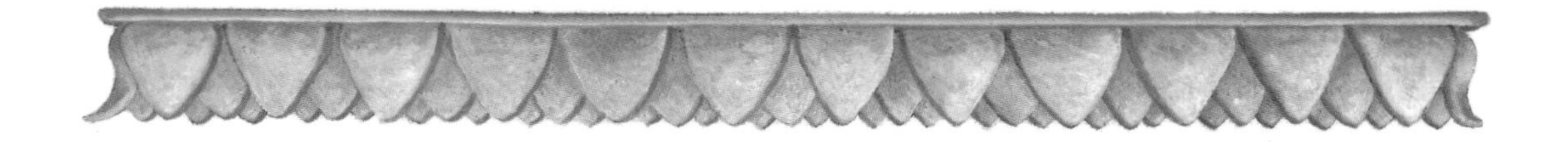

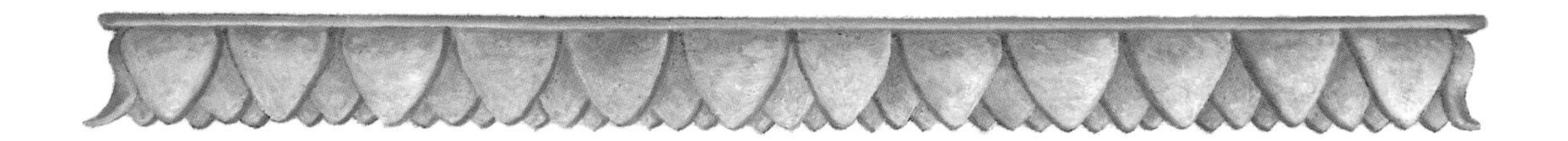

Abdul thought he should make a little speech the way the king's grandson Henry had. But the words wouldn't come.

Finally, Abdul looked at the king and said simply, "*Oh là là!*"

It seemed to be the right thing to say, for the king began to rub his hands together just as the pasha had when he was satisfied. "Perfect," the king said. "A perfect ending to a perfect day."

Although it is hard to know for sure what giraffes are thinking, because they are silent creatures, one thing was certain. The king's giraffe was never lonely in his new home. That first summer alone more than six hundred thousand people came to see him. He was loved and admired, and he made people happy. The giraffe lived with the Royal Menagerie until 1845, and Abdul stayed with him all those many years.

When it came time to send to Africa for another giraffe, the people of France decided that their first giraffe had been so special that he could never be replaced, and so they left his cage empty. By this time he was a legend. Books were written about him. Paintings were made and songs were sung about him.

Abdul stayed in Paris in the little stone cottage that the king had had built for him in the Jardin des Plantes, near the Royal Menagerie. Each spring, after the harsh wind had blown its way through the south of France, he would take a trip to Marseilles to visit the mayor, who was now the ex-mayor, and his wife. Then Abdul would head back to Paris following the route that he had traveled with his giraffe, stopping in each town and village to reflect on that extraordinary journey that he had made so long ago.

At times it all seemed like a dream to Abdul. But he knew it had really happened because all along the route he took from Marseilles to Paris,

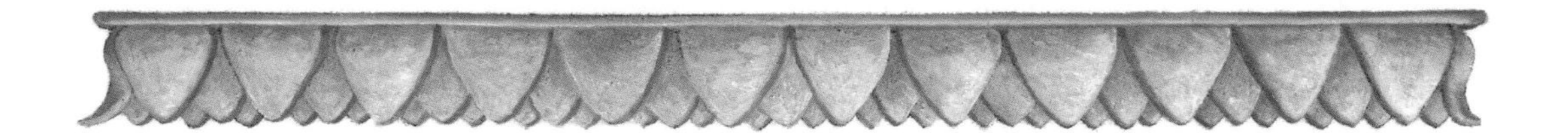

in each town and village through which he passed, there were still landmarks: streets named Rue de la Girafe or squares called Place de la Girafe. You can still find them there today, proof of how much the people of France appreciated the very special gift sent to them from Africa by Mehemet Ali, the pasha of Egypt.